ALSO BY CHRISTINE COULSON

Metropolitan Stories

ONE WOMAN SHOW

A Novel

Christine Coulson

AVID READER PRESS

New York   London   Toronto   Sydney   New Delhi

Avid Reader Press
An Imprint of Simon & Schuster, Inc.
1230 Avenue of the Americas
New York, NY 10020

First Avid Reader Press hardcover edition October 2023

AVID READER PRESS and colophon are trademarks of Simon & Schuster, Inc.

For information about special discounts for bulk purchases, please contact Simon & Schuster Special Sales at 1-866-506-1949 or business@simonandschuster.com.

The Simon & Schuster Speakers Bureau can bring authors to your live event. For more information or to book an event, contact the Simon & Schuster Speakers Bureau at 1-866-248-3049 or visit our website at www.simonspeakers.com.

Interior design by Carly Loman

Manufactured in the United States of America

10   9   8   7   6   5   4   3   2   1

Library of Congress Cataloging-in-Publication Data

Names: Coulson, Christine, author.
Title: One woman show : a novel / Christine Coulson.
Description: First Avid Reader Press hardcover edition. | New York : Avid Reader Press, 2023.
Identifiers: LCCN 2023011665 (print) | LCCN 2023011666 (ebook) | ISBN 9781668027783 (hardcover) | ISBN 9781668027790 (paperback) | ISBN 9781668027806 (ebook)
Subjects: LCGFT: Novels.
Classification: LCC PS3603.O885 O54 2023 (print) | LCC PS3603.O885 (ebook) | DDC 813/.6--dc23/eng/20230317
LC record available at https://lccn.loc.gov/2023011665
LC ebook record available at https://lccn.loc.gov/2023011666

ISBN 978-1-6680-2778-3
ISBN 978-1-6680-2780-6 (ebook)

For C. C. & C.

Always stop for beauty.

gar·ni·ture (gär-ni-chər), *n.* a set of decorative objects (such as vases or urns)

ONE WOMAN SHOW

Opening October 17, 2023

*This exhibition is made possible by gin, taffeta, and stock dividends.
Additional support has been provided by quiet fortitude
and a sly, necessary wit.*

MASTERPIECE, AGED 5, 1911

Caroline Margaret Brooks Whitaker (known as Kitty), b. 1906
Collection of Martha and Harrison Whitaker (known as Minty and Whit)

With arms folded in deliberate contrapposto, Minty and Whit Whitaker observe their daughter, Kitty, positioned in a strip of expensive morning sunlight. The five-year-old knows she is being watched and adjusts herself to advantage. Her glaze glows, enhanced flawlessly by her subtle sculptural design. She is all fireworks, this golden child, a delirious display of Bernini verve and unrivaled WASP artistry.

MANHATTAN CHILD, AGED 6, 1912
Caroline Margaret Brooks Whitaker (known as Kitty)
Collection of Martha and Harrison Whitaker

Kitty and the related examples in her garniture follow the precedent of earlier forms, ignoring the avant-garde of contemporary European movements like Cubism in deference to careful restraint and balanced presentation. Like many society standards of similar manufacture, Kitty's smooth surfaces and refined proportions borrow from the eighteenth-century example of Robert Adam's neoclassical designs. In a small rococo flourish, Kitty likes to steal things.

R. HARRISON BOBBINGTON WHITAKER (KNOWN AS WHIT)
Kitty's Father, Aged 31, 1912
Ex–Collection of Frances and Barnaby Whitaker (known as Flit
and Bobby)

Formed in the Anglophilic taste, Whit Whitaker toggles gently
between dandy and daddy. The eldest of four known works
from the earlier Whitaker collection, this jardiniere is designed
to hold and propagate the Whitaker paper fortune. Embracing
a broad range of florid design gestures, he displays a marked
preference for the company of younger men. The distinctly
handsome qualities of his wife, Minty, are often remarked upon
with more than a hint of insinuation.

MARTHA JANE THOMPSON BROOKS WHITAKER (KNOWN AS MINTY)
Kitty's Mother, Aged 29, 1912
Ex–Collection of Prudence and Eliot Hay Brooks (known as Bunty and Eli)

A monument to classical rigor, Minty Whitaker improbably personifies the stylistic imperatives of discipline and desire. Eschewing standard modes of adornment, she is purely *Mayflower* made—all guile, no gilding—making her cash-hungry pairing with Whit Whitaker a predictable coupling of pedigree and prosperity. Minty's severity and austere silhouette distract from her more lascivious cravings, which consistently extend beyond traditionally acceptable levels.

RIVAL, AGED 7, 1913
Caroline Margaret Brooks Whitaker (known as Kitty)
Collection of Martha and Harrison Whitaker

An awareness of curatorial hierarchy arrives early as Kitty
recognizes the limited real estate of any prized pedestal.
Critical distinctions are being made, judgments imposed, and
rankings adjusted by a collective force that Kitty feels but does
not quite understand. Her fellow garniture members all bear
the weight of this competition from a young age, the sense of
being evaluated to determine who will be the most treasured
object among them.

FIRST GRADER, THE CHAPIN SCHOOL, AGED 7, 1914
Caroline Margaret Brooks Whitaker (known as Kitty)
Collection of Martha and Harrison Whitaker

A model of childhood cruelty, Kitty joyfully locks her friend
Whippy Stokes in a Louis XVI commode. While Kitty sits atop
the cabinet carelessly admiring its gilt ormolu, Whippy begs
to be set free in a tiny, imperceptible voice. Eventually, a thin
stream of Whippy's pee trickles from beneath the cupboard
doors. Whippy is shattered, her wet legs matching her damp,
flushed cheeks. Above, Kitty remains pertly arranged, arms
akimbo, lips protruding, and gleams just a little brighter.

UPPER EAST SIDE GIRL, AGED 10, 1916
Caroline Margaret Brooks Whitaker (known as Kitty)
Collection of Martha and Harrison Whitaker

Glitter and gloss define the vitrine of a Park Avenue life, and
Kitty plays the role of trifle with gusto. She charms guests at
tea with porcelain manners, rippling with charisma like gilding
along a rim. But a hum of humiliation jitters below the surface
of this exhibition. Even at age ten, Kitty senses a suffocating
tyranny on the horizon. Not the war in Europe, but the fragile
need to be forever cared for according to someone else's tastes
and appetites.

WORD COLLECTOR, AGED 10, 1917
Caroline Margaret Brooks Whitaker (known as Kitty)
Collection of Martha and Harrison Whitaker

Kitty transcribes beloved words in a miniature notebook
the size of a medieval Book of Hours. The result is a Dada
manifesto, carefully inscribed with calligraphic flair: *loquacious,
indubitably, mellifluous, cataclysm, indefatigable.* Much like
stealing, this secret gathering of small things from their broader
context soothes in its peculiar way. *Languor, propinquity, raven,
bamboozle.* Unlike stealing, these words lack the gentle frisson
of transgression. The list is soon updated to include *copulation*
and *boob.*

FRESHMAN, MISS PORTER'S SCHOOL, FARMINGTON, CT, AGED 13, 1920
Caroline Margaret Brooks Whitaker (known as Kitty)
Collection of Martha and Harrison Whitaker

Despite Kitty's delicate glaze, exaggerated gilding, and genteel curvature, a lisp clouds her early years. "Thorry," Kitty repeats again and again with each fumbled turn of phrase. Determined to overcome this imperfection when she arrives at boarding school, thirteen-year-old Kitty trains her muscles to clamp her jaw, sending words into the world through locked teeth, and with a rigid determination never to let her tongue yield again. For anything.

NUDE CARYATID, MISS PORTER'S SCHOOL, AGED 14, 1921
Caroline Margaret Brooks Whitaker (known as Kitty)
Collection of Martha and Harrison Whitaker

Applying archaic production methods, Miss Porter's School
cultivates the figural composition of its students through the
practice of balancing books upon their heads—while naked.
During an annual inspection, Kitty pulls her torso upright and
quivers to support her neck, head, and three volumes of Balzac.
A yardstick measures each student's height as a flashbulb
pops to document her progress. This registrarial protocol is
abandoned in 1935 when a stash of these nude photographs is
discovered in a janitor's office.

SOPHOMORE, MISS PORTER'S SCHOOL, AGED 15, 1922
Caroline Margaret Brooks Whitaker (known as Kitty)
Collection of Martha and Harrison Whitaker

A private self-assessment in Kitty's closet reveals imbalance
in her classical form. Typical for the period, Mannerist curves
now swell her once-columnar figure. She turns her cheek
and presses her chest against the wall hoping to sink the egg
and dart moldings of her breasts back into their sockets. She
imagines the return of her lithe body with its uninterrupted
silhouette, while a salt glaze of tears stains the back of her hand.

JUNIOR, MISS PORTER'S SCHOOL, AGED 16, 1922
Caroline Margaret Brooks Whitaker (known as Kitty)
Collection of Martha and Harrison Whitaker

Inventory reveals that Kitty is no longer in her vitrine. Security officers search every shelf in Farmington, Connecticut, to find Kitty mislabeled in a local shop and filled with pilfered candy. She is returned with white-gloved precision along with a condition report that reveals no significant damage. Kitty's precedent will have a profound impact on collection management and inspires a generation of lesser imitations.

DREAMER, AGED 17, 1924
Caroline Margaret Brooks Whitaker (known as Kitty)
Collection of Martha and Harrison Whitaker

The Surrealist movement takes hold in Europe, and Kitty
considers her own dreams. She imagines herself running,
tumbling, moving faster and forward from something—
from herself, on her shelf—spilling into some boundless void.
All her fantasies involve freedom, all her desires spin from
the seduction of compositional instability, a fierce longing
to be distinctly *un*-decorative in the tradition of Artemisia
Gentileschi's heroic femininity. Instead, she must write her
mother to thank her for her new winter coat.

FRESHMAN, SMITH COLLEGE, NORTHAMPTON, MA, AGED 17, 1924
Caroline Margaret Brooks Whitaker (known as Kitty)
Collection of Martha and Harrison Whitaker

Kitty is placed with a new garniture at Smith College. With clichéd predictability, her studio purity falls away and is replaced with a composition of fresh dynamism. She smokes, bobs her hair, studies art history, and French-kisses Amelia Lockwood, who plays the harpsichord and wears a monocle. A Rose Period of stealth rebellion ensues in this new, privileged bohemia. Each dawn delivers another sensation, another madness, another craving to be breathlessly pursued.

FIANCÉE, AGED 18, 1925
Caroline Margaret Brooks Whitaker (known as Kitty)
Collection of Martha and Harrison Whitaker

The swirling Rose Period of collegiate passion and endeavor ends prematurely when Kitty is exhibited at an Egyptian-themed spring cotillion in 1925. William "Bucky" Wallingford III, the mining pharaoh of Pittsburgh, notices Kitty's fine profile among the Tut-inspired sphinxes and hieroglyphs. The boy king proposes by summer's end and Cleopatra Kitty accepts. She leaves Smith's halcyon glow behind, but is electrified by the prospect of being installed as the centerpiece of this new dynastic collection.

"Well, we've done it, darling," Minty Whitaker sighed. "She'll be down the aisle in a matter of hours."

"I've worried about that ungainly thing since the day she was born," Whit replied. "Remember how she used to preen for us on the floor, so awkward with that lisp? How many times I thought to myself, she literally looks like something we found in the basement."

"Now, dear, we have raised a fine young lady," Minty said. "She's just a bit . . . eccentric."

"Well, thank goodness that Pittsburgh fortune needs a nudge up," Whit said. "Taste is a fickle creature, but provenance, well, that's all the beauty you need sometimes."

BRIDE, AGED 19, 1926
Mrs. William Wallingford III (known as Kitty)
Collection of William Wallingford III (known as Bucky)
Ex–Collection of Martha and Harrison Whitaker

Considered the apex of early twentieth-century production,
Kitty is thoroughly polished, bound in white silk, and decorated
with a clutch of pristine lily of the valley. The rest of her
garniture joins her, but with deliberately less polish and
packaging. The great and the good gather to see the exhibition
and rave about elegant lines and immaculate condition. Kitty
glistens in the light of her new pedestal and foolishly considers
herself now unbreakable.

MELISSA KILMAN CODDINGTON CRANE (KNOWN AS SISSY)

Bridesmaid #1, Aged 19, 1926

Collection of Clarissa and Buford Crane (known as Clara and Biff)

On loan

A member of Kitty's original garniture, Sissy engages in the unfamiliar work of standing as accessory to Kitty's centerpiece. She has long considered Kitty of inferior provenance despite their equally balanced proportions and related manufacture. Their formal relationship is one of obligation, ornamented with competition and a hint of unsettled history. They reunite for this exhibition, but Sissy secretly longs to elbow Kitty off the shelf.

WHITNEY LONGHILL STOKES (KNOWN AS WHIPPY)
Bridesmaid #2, Aged 19, 1926
Collection of Mary and Bingham Stokes (known as Molly and Ham)
On loan

Whippy is perplexed by Kitty's compositional placement at the center of their garniture. Iconographically, she understands the bridal construct and its medieval traditions, but under strict formal analysis Whippy knows that her hair is much shinier than Kitty's. And Whippy has a pony.

HARRIET PARKER CARTWRIGHT (KNOWN AS CORKIE)
Bridesmaid #3, Aged 19, 1926
Collection of Edith and Winthrop Cartwright III (known as
Edie and Topper)
On loan

The broad proportions of a Romanesque silhouette delineate
Corkie, who believes her excessive wealth will always ensure
her position at the center of Kitty's garniture. Cartwright
banking profits have inflated to Medici proportions, leaving
Corkie baffled by Kitty's triumph and her own demotion within
their compositional arrangement. After too much gin, Corkie
leaves the wedding with a waiter who claims to be a Symbolist
poet and mime.

CECILIA JOAN HUNTINGTON (KNOWN AS CECE)
Bridesmaid #4, Aged 19, 1926
Collection of Margaret and Russell Huntington (known as
Gogo and Sully)
On loan

Differing from her garniture companions, Cece is firmly assured
of her centerpiece status for having rejected the groom before
he met Kitty. The arabesque motifs of Bucky's Pittsburgh
prosperity could not lure Cece's delicate scrolls. She maintains
conventions of the period by remaining subordinate within the
overall bridal configuration, while knowing that hierarchically
she is definitively superior. Upon their reunion, Bucky
introduces himself as if they have never met.

WILLIAM WALLINGFORD III (KNOWN AS BUCKY)
Kitty's First Husband, Aged 22, 1926
Collection of Cornelia and William Wallingford, Jr. (known as
Elsie and Bill)

An early work in the Wallingford collection, Bucky upholds
a singular blend of naturalism and idealization with innate
good looks and a colossal fortune. His stylized elegance defies
his Pittsburgh provenance and demonstrates the integration
of Northeastern influences from Choate and Yale. Evidence
of these compositional changes has no discernible effect
on Bucky's lumbering intellect and tapering worldview. He
remains an adored fixture, a confection in the tradition of a
Meissen monkey table ornament.

"Should we have a whole garniture of babies? A plethora? A surfeit? A profusion?" Kitty babbled on their wedding night after the wrapping had come off, the spotlight dimmed, and her vessel duly filled.

"Well, if you mean a pair of boys, then sure," Bucky replied. "You're a funny girl, Mrs. Wallingford, a funny girl. Someday, I might really like you."

"Yep," Kitty said into the dark, "but then it might be too late."

PORTRAIT SUBJECT, AGED 20, 1927
Mrs. William Wallingford III (known as Kitty)
Collection of William Wallingford III
Ex–Collection of Martha and Harrison Whitaker
Traveling exhibition

Kitty upholds the formal continuity of the gold-rimmed
American in Paris, arriving during her yearlong honeymoon
to be painted by Romaine Brooks in fashionable androgyny.
The shift from fixed and stolid Park Avenue to this new venue
of crackling intellect lends fresh context to Kitty's classicism,
binding her to an alluring, though unspoken, feminist strength.
Such avant-garde influence will be fleeting when Kitty's New
York life continues within the confines of its pillowed vitrine.

"How Kitty tried, but she could be nothing but American," Romaine recalled to Lady Troubridge.

"She reminds me of those dreadful English vases covered in swags and gilding 'in the French taste,' " Lady Troubridge replied.

"What a curious contradiction to steal every detail from the French and somehow achieve an effect that is completely foreign to France," Romaine continued. "I also think she took my pocket watch."

ROSARIO CANDELA (1890–1953)
Floorplan of 990 Fifth Avenue, Floors 10 and 11
Ink on paper, 1927
Collection of Avery Architectural and Fine Arts Library,
Columbia University, New York, NY (AA685.16)

Recent acquisitions often require reframing, and Kitty demands
no less of her post-nuptial installation. Architect Rosario
Candela has recently unveiled 990 Fifth Avenue, where the
Bucky Wallingfords build their Middle Kingdom among the
boiserie. Georges Braque's Cubist still life, a wedding gift from
Kitty's in-laws, hangs over the fireplace. Kitty prefers Picasso
for sex appeal and name recognition but hides her thundering
discontent with a practiced display of neon joy.

GEORGES BRAQUE (1882–1963)
Still Life
Oil, charcoal, and sand on canvas, 1914
Collection of Mr. and Mrs. William Wallingford III
Ex–Collection of Galerie Kahnweiler, Paris

A Cubist masterpiece, this still life is a monument to the
revolutionary artistic style pioneered by Braque and Picasso
beginning in 1907. Multiple views of the same objects are
united in a single picture plane, fragmenting the image with
shifting and repetitive forms. The space remains compressed
within the surface of the canvas, as the central table tilts
forward to reveal the patterned shapes that compose the still-
life arrangement, interrupted by the partially obscured words
Quotidien and *Café*.

"Kitty's a little weird, you know," Bucky confessed to his father. "She's always using these complicated words. Pernicious. And verisimilitude. Very similar to what?? Sometimes I catch her posing as if . . . hell, I don't really know what she's doing. . . ."

"Son," Bill Wallingford replied slowly, "a girl like Kitty's what you'd call an acquired taste. You know, your mother made us buy that crazy painting in Paris for your wedding present. We walked into this place that she'd found and I didn't care for any of it. Every painting was a mess, all these muddy shapes, and your mother was just over the moon for the stuff, so we bought one and gave it to you and you hung it over the fireplace and that will be that. Probably not worth the canvas it's painted on. Kitty's the same way: Mother thinks she's marvelous—you know your mother is desperate for a Mayflower connection—so we got her, and you married her and we put her in the apartment and that will be that. That's your verisimilitude. It's very similar to everyone else, so just get used to it."

LOUISE GREENE
Maid, Aged 46, 1927
Provenance unknown
On loan

On loan from Kitty's mother, the neat and spare Mrs. Greene
monitors Kitty with perplexed fascination. Kitty's state is
perpetually performative, as if an audience is poised to admire
her at every moment. Following the archetype of Narcissus,
Kitty seems thoroughly consumed by her own reflection
and the fashionable placement of her form within her finely
appointed interior. Mrs. Greene sees her as just another surface
to be dusted, perhaps polished, perhaps with white gloves, but
really, only dusted.

WIFE, AGED 21, 1927
Mrs. William Wallingford III (known as Kitty)
Collection of William Wallingford III
Ex–Collection of Martha and Harrison Whitaker

Now a coveted pair, Bucky and Kitty shine among the finest
of examples of WASP artistic production. They anchor the
collection of eminently marriageable people who populate
Fifth Avenue dinner parties and cocktail gatherings in smart,
mid-block buildings in the East 60s. Coupling ravenously in
gin-soaked delirium anywhere they can—closets, pantries, atop
mahogany Chippendale—they seem to know instinctively
that their brittle Puritan material will eventually resist such
deliberately intertwined filigree.

COUNTRY KITTY, AGED 21, 1927
Mrs. William Wallingford III (known as Kitty)
Collection of William Wallingford III
Ex–Collection of Martha and Harrison Whitaker

A reflected palette of green and brown replaces the city's
grisaille glaze when Kitty is occasionally brought to the
Wallingfords' country residence in Connecticut. Kitty finds
pastoral life tedious and lacking. The audience is flimsy, and the
activities perilous to her fragile form. Despite prevailing WASP
conventions, Kitty prefers the serenity of the indoors, soothed
by insect-free conditions and the tender security of an encased
circumstance.

DISPLAY MODEL, AGED 21, 1928
Mrs. William Wallingford III (known as Kitty)
Collection of William Wallingford III
Ex–Collection of Martha and Harrison Whitaker

A masterwork of aesthetic and nuptial achievement, Kitty glows in triumphant splendor. Light bounces buoyantly from her every surface as if she were a child again, the focus of her parents' adoring gaze. With astonishing facility, Kitty ignites the illusion of buzzing occupation, beguiling viewers while she blithely does absolutely nothing.

MOTHER, AGED 21, 1928
Mrs. William Wallingford III (known as Kitty)
Collection of William Wallingford III
Ex–Collection of Martha and Harrison Whitaker

With stopwatch precision, a Baroque swell of fertility secures
Kitty's place as a traditional vessel. But studio malfunctions
propel the glossy pink snuffbox through Kitty as if she were
constructed of lace. The baby survives for the sole beat
of Kitty's whispered, possessive greeting, "mine," before
vanishing like an erased line. Kitty's Blue Period begins. Like
a faint fissure from within, the clutching memory of those
few seconds will break Kitty below the surface, a persistent
interruption beneath her varnish.

"*The sooner that we can overcome our grief and turn our thoughts to the future, the better. Because mourning is a continual reminder of the past, it can only delay one's return to a normal life.*"

Emily Post, *Etiquette*, 1927

DINNER GUEST, AGED 22, 1928
Mrs. William Wallingford III (known as Kitty)
Collection of William Wallingford III
Ex–Collection of Martha and Harrison Whitaker

Feigning restoration, Kitty returns to adorn obligatory social rituals. Her first showing is a dinner party at the home of Mrs. Clarence Duckworth, a lugubrious teapot of a woman known to indulge very little ornament. Kitty's luster remains impenetrable, but she drinks with vigor, repeatedly filling her vessel as if to test its new fractures.

CLAIRE GENEVIEVE WILMOT DUCKWORTH (KNOWN AS GINNY)
Dinner Party Hostess, Aged 36, 1928
Collection of Clarence Buford Duckworth (known as Duckie)

A prominent example of oppression in the domestic interior, Ginny seizes upon her guests as if they were fresh military recruits. Her directives are at once animating and paralyzing, quickly removing any hint of impulsivity from her proceedings. As the evening's cocktails take hold, she perches skittishly at the end of her table like the dictator of a small, unruly nation, eyes bouncing between her guests to prevent a gin-fueled coup d'état.

"Why, thank you, I don't know why I'm so awfully thirsty this evening, but yes, another gin would be lovely. . . . A corker, me? Why, of course you can keep up; you can't let me drink all by myself. That would just be rude, and then old Mrs. Duckworth would worry we're not having a good time—Yes, maybe just a drop more. Can't have you drinking alone either. . . . Now, which one's your wife? Oh, Mugsie! Yes, of course. She is handsome, isn't she. And not in that boyish, rotten way, but like a stylish mère supérieure—without the vow of chastity, I hope! Ha! . . . Pennsylvania, you say? My Bucky's from Pittsburgh. . . . Steel mines, stuffed with cash. Last generation didn't have a pot to piss in and now—boom—he's like a boy king— Oh, maybe just one more glass— Oh hi! Here's my Bucky! Yes, darling?. . . Your lamb? Yes, I suppose I am your lamb. What are we girls but farm animals once we get married off? Though, in my case, with no other lambs in the barn— Leave now? But you haven't even met Mr. Sutton— Oh, it's Mutton, you say? Silly me. So, your wife is Mugsie Mutton? Well, that's a sheep of a whole other sort. Mugsie Mutton! What a hoot! Like an ovine gangster. A hoot! . . . Ugh, I know when I'm licked. Excuse me, Mr. Sutton, Mutton. You are a thrill, I tell you. A real thrill. Now take that bootlegger wife of yours out dancing. Oh, darling Bucky, you silly little fool, should we go out dancing with the Sutton Muttons? Wouldn't that be a hoot?"

WHITNEY STOKES VANDERLOO (KNOWN AS WHIPPY)
Former Bridesmaid/Crash Casualty, Aged 23, 1929
Collection of Lincoln Taylor Vanderloo (known as Link)
Ex–Collection of Mary and Bingham Stokes

Contemporary accounts record Whippy's fall from the garniture
installation. A historic crash wipes out the Stokes and Vanderloo
fortunes, leaving only shards. Restoration seems improbable as
conservators work frantically and futilely to address stockpiles
of similar losses in collections throughout the nation. Basic
decorative motifs must now be reorganized to accommodate
this shocking new reality. The break marks a fundamental
disruption in the garniture's compositional certainty and a
permanent shift in Whippy's exhibition status.

LICKER, AGED 24, 1931
Mrs. William Wallingford III (known as Kitty)
Collection of William Wallingford III
Ex–Collection of Martha and Harrison Whitaker

Society's Depression-era thrift leaves Kitty's decorative
qualities neglected for more utilitarian forms. Lacking the
audience of social life, she becomes furtively decadent, eating
thickly frosted cakes into which she has pressed her own
jewels. After the cake is devoured, she licks the frosting from
her sugar-encrusted parure with abandon, while worrying that
such bustling tongue activity could cause her lisp to return. It
is the eve of her twenty-fifth birthday when she first tugs at her
face and wonders if it's time for new gilding.

DREAM BABIES, 1929–1933
Collection of Mrs. William Wallingford III

Presaging later artistic movements of similar personal intensity, the crimson pigment that gushes forth from Kitty's interior signals a shattering within her vessel. These stains differ markedly from the monthly abstractions that interrupt silk undergarments with symbols of youth and fertility. Present when expected to be absent, this red compositional disruption indicates a forfeiture too often endured. As Kitty's collection of vanishing babies multiplies, the realization arrives that many things she considered inevitable and certain are not.

PETTY THIEF, AGED 27, 1933
Mrs. William Wallingford III (known as Kitty)
Collection of William Wallingford III
Ex–Collection of Martha and Harrison Whitaker

With increasing mastery, Kitty quietly appropriates small tokens
of novel ornament from a range of sources. A fountain pen,
a silver fork, a green glass marble, a hatpin in the shape of a
miniature owl, collected as if they were Grand Tour souvenirs.
Each object follows another bloodstained loss within her vessel
at the peak of its production. Each theft brings unexplained
relief.

"You all right, Kitty?" Bucky asked, surprised by how fond he had grown of his peculiar wife. His father had been right.

"Your propinquity is all I need, Mr. Wallingford."

"Well, you've got it, Mrs. Wallingford. And I don't even know what propinsity means. But if that's all you need, then that's what I've got."

"I think maybe it's going to be just us, Bucky. No surfeit of babies after all."

"Maybe just us is just fine. Who needs surfing babies anyway?"

WAR WIFE, AGED 35, 1942
Mrs. William Wallingford III (known as Kitty)
Collection of William Wallingford III
Ex–Collection of Martha and Harrison Whitaker

Dust has settled on the once-shimmering pair. Museums close
at the dawn of war, anxious that an attack might threaten their
treasures. Kitty goes into storage while her husband is shipped
to Europe. The dark unknowing frightens her and, for once,
she is grateful to be childless. Her glaze fractures in the chill
of crippling loneliness, and an irreparable craquelure spreads
across her surface like grasping fingers. Bucky will not return,
another brutal blow to Kitty's structural integrity.

STILL LIFE, AGED 35–38, 1942–1945
Mrs. William Wallingford III (known as Kitty)
Ex–Collection of Martha and Harrison Whitaker; William
Wallingford III
Off-view

Echoing the solemn compositions of Cézanne, Kitty remains
static, stiffened by the brutality of death's restricted palette.
The deliberate structure of mourning encourages further
constraint as war quells modern life's dash and spontaneity.
Kitty's pulse beats with memories of lighter days, both radiant
and weightless. She is stilled by the knowledge that she will
emerge from this isolation a one woman show.

"While a garniture is lovely and certainly appropriate in many a sitting room, porcelain is always most desirable in pairs. Only a true masterpiece can stand alone."

Bitsy Plimpton, in her lecture "Decorating for You" delivered at the Colony Club, 1945

WIDOW, AGED 39, 1946
Mrs. William Wallingford III (known as Kitty)
Ex–Collection of Martha and Harrison Whitaker; William
Wallingford III

Post-war Kitty maintains her neoclassical form through a
regimen of cigarettes, coffee, and grapefruit. She has been
separated from her original garniture for more than two decades
and has found an alternative coupling from a royal Portuguese
manufactory. A handsome, collectible pair, despite their stylistic
disparities, tonal variations, seething anger, and significant need
for restoration. Luiz drinks, while Kitty plays bridge and ignores
his increasingly visible damage.

SECOND-TIME BRIDE, AGED 40, 1947

Mrs. Luiz de Braganza (known as Kitty)
Collection of Luiz Carlos Alfonso Antonio de Braganza
Ex–Collection of Martha and Harrison Whitaker; William
Wallingford III

According to conventions of the period, no orange blossom or
myrtle wreath decorates this second-time bride and her absent
virginity. The bridesmaid garniture is likewise jettisoned for a
solo presentation. Kitty and Luiz marry at 990 Fifth Avenue for
convenience and discretion, inviting a modest group of people
who silently note the dueling opulence and melancholy. It is
more installation than exhibition this time around, and the
chiaroscuro lighting does not flatter.

LUIZ CARLOS ALFONSO ANTONIO DE BRAGANZA
Kitty's Second Husband, Aged 53, 1947
Ex–Collection of Maria Luiza and Alfonso de Braganza

Generally considered a prestige object, Luiz exhibits all the sumptuous characteristics of royal manufacture. His gold ground hosts swags of lively ornament that distract from deep reserves of cocktail despair. Regal provenance and spiraling wit publicly obscure noteworthy condition issues, despite their exaggerated presence in the raking light of a domestic setting. Mutually burnished by status, Kitty and Luiz form a powerful allegory of cachet coupling in post-war New York.

"He's a swarthy thing, isn't he?"

"Oh please, Corkie. Don't sound so provincial."

"I'm not provincial. I'm just saying he's . . . exotic."

"A lot can be forgiven for a prince, my dear."

"Do we know he's a prince?"

"Well, he's certainly handsome for a foreigner. It would be marvelous if he were a spy."

"Oh, good lord, Binky Winthrop just handed him her empty glass as if he were a waiter."

"Be a good boy and get me a refill," Binky barked.

SURGICAL PATIENT, AGED 42, 1949
Mrs. Luiz de Braganza (known as Kitty)
Collection of Luiz Carlos Alfonso Antonio de Braganza
Ex–Collection of Martha and Harrison Whitaker; William
Wallingford III

Sensitive conservation is less about what one does than when
one stops. A network of fine cracks known as crazing has
expanded across Kitty's surface, which is consolidated and
lifted before it is too late. Restoration pulls this outer glaze
taut, leaving behind a mask anchored below the ear and at
the temples like a shirred pouch of muscle and bone. Regular
applications of decorative paint will be needed to draw the eye
elsewhere.

LOUISE GREENE
Maid, Aged 68, 1949
Provenance unknown
Purchase, Martha and Harrison Whitaker Fund, 1928

Fluent in the demands of diligent maintenance, Mrs. Greene
reluctantly admires Kitty during her restoration period.
The refined simplicity of her freshly conserved decoration
does capture the vitality of its precedent, that earlier child
of such ebullient vanity and idle. Confounding that artistic
achievement are the stolen baubles of various forms that
Mrs. Greene apathetically dusts each week. After twenty years
of steady connoisseurship, Mrs. Greene is sure of only one
thing: There is no stranger display than a bored, rich, porcelain
girl.

TUNA SALAD ON WHITE TOAST WITH CARROT STICKS
Lunch, 1950
Collection of William Poll Specialty Foods & Catering,
1051 Lexington Avenue, New York City

A rectilinear composition of four diminutive sandwich triangles
punctuates a circular porcelain plate in an abstract portrait
of caloric constraint. Three orange stripes, peeled carrots of
limited dimension, add to the Mondrian rigor, drawing the
eye without tempting the palate. Kitty eats this still life alone
and with the quiet resolve of a squirrel unable to temper the
determined lust of its consumption. A cigarette follows.

SOCIETY FORCE, AGED 43, 1950

Mrs. Luiz de Braganza (known as Kitty)

Collection of Luiz Carlos Alfonso Antonio de Braganza

Ex–Collection of Martha and Harrison Whitaker; William Wallingford III

Kitty dazzles with high glamour, crushing the garniture accessories in ballrooms all over town. A stricter, energized line brings renewed interest to her starved silhouette, inspiring School of Kitty followers to endure punishing hunger for such visual punctuation. Viewers find Kitty's Gothic revival simultaneously riveting and monstrous. Kitty, buoyant in a haze of ravishing deprivation, finds *them* tiresome. And fat.

"Bucky actually wanted to marry Cece, not Kitty."

"You know Kitty's father is Jewish."

"He is not Jewish. But she was a lesbian for a while."

"Everyone was a lesbian for a while."

"Little Kitty Whitaker was no lesbian."

"Whatever the hell she was, she's queen now."

"And unbreakable in that gown."

"Unbreakable."

BULLFIGHTER, AGED 44, 1950

Mrs. Luiz de Braganza (known as Kitty)
Collection of Luiz Carlos Alfonso Antonio de Braganza
Ex–Collection of Martha and Harrison Whitaker; William
Wallingford III
Traveling exhibition

Rejecting the vernacular during a visit to London, Kitty
champions the canon in a discreet assignation with Picasso
during the second of his two trips to England. The artist's
legendary appetites are no match for Kitty in full force. She
seduces with industry and abandon, replacing traditional modes
of expression with robust techniques based on curvilinear
forms. Picasso, awed by the stark and savage edges beneath
Kitty's gilding, handles her as if she were made of bronze.

"Does it look like me?" Kitty asked sarcastically as she posed naked, smoking a cigarette.

"Look like you? No. It is *you."*

BROKEN, AGED 47, 1954
Mrs. Luiz de Braganza (known as Kitty)
Collection of Luiz Carlos Alfonso Antonio de Braganza
Ex–Collection of Martha and Harrison Whitaker; William
Wallingford III

Following earlier precedents of royal provenance, Luiz bridges
the gap between rococo indolence and modernist rage. His
highly polished veneer cannot conceal the violent carcass
to which it is attached. In a period of byzantine wrath, Kitty
joltingly tumbles from his grasp and suffers significant abrasions
to her varnish. Corrective retouching does little to distract Kitty
from the shrewd planning of a revived solo exhibition.

DIVORCÉE, AGED 50, 1956
Mrs. Caroline de Braganza (known as Kitty)
Ex–Collection of Martha and Harrison Whitaker; William
Wallingford III; Luiz Carlos Alfonso Antonio de Braganza

Earlier ornament has been rediscovered under Kitty's glaze. At
eighteen, Kitty's decoration was pierced in the bathroom at an
Amherst College dance. The Portuguese companion has been
deaccessioned, and Kitty dreams about the handsome source
of that first incision. Should he be the one beside her as she
ages on the shelf? She may soon be out of fashion in an Abstract
Expressionist world, and male inventory is dwindling.

"*Whatever happened to Chippy Hastings? Anyone know?*" Kitty asked the group lightly.

"*Chippy? Haven't thought of him in years. Did you go out with him before Bucky?*"

"*He took me to a dance at Amherst once . . . probably 1924,*" Kitty said, smirking faintly as she thought about her clumsy enthusiasm that night.

"*Oh, Chippy . . . wasn't he divine? Such a dear. He dated my sister, Beedie, for a while. Didn't come back from the war.*"

"*Uh, how inconvenient,*" Kitty mumbled to herself, then looked up again at the group. "*Remember the days when we were promised a world of lean, easy men,*" she continued with a reverie that silenced the others, "*and we thought it would be forever, for the rest of our lives? Where are they all now, those boys, our promised swains? They can't all be dead.*"

THIRD-TIME BRIDE, AGED 51, 1957
Mrs. George Deen (known as Kitty)
Collection of George Robert Hoppington Deen
Ex–Collection of Martha and Harrison Whitaker; William
Wallingford III; Luiz Carlos Alfonso Antonio de Braganza

With little fanfare, a recent acquisition is installed in Kitty's
vitrine to stabilize her solo composition. Returning to carefully
balanced classicism, George Deen's adjacency revives Kitty. It
is a tepid renaissance, devoid of artistic bravado or elaborate
gestures, but one that repairs Kitty's withering loneliness,
a solitude that recalls her wartime storage. Again, it is the
pedestal of marriage that soothes and saves, offering the
consoling comfort of a familiar floorplan.

GEORGE ROBERT HOPPINGTON DEEN
Kitty's Third Husband, Aged 62, 1957
Ex–Collection of Alice and Henry Hoppington Deen (known as
Pokey and Hank)

Essentially formed in the jocular idiom, George is traditionally
rendered in the manner of companionable third husbands.
While not the fizz of any party, he is a welcome guest, an
enduring accessory to Kitty's ever more callous temperament.
Like a sterling silver knife rest, he serves as a decorative prop
to support an increasingly sharp slicing instrument.

"Did you really have an affair with Picasso, Kitty?" George asked his new wife one evening.

"Oh, I do love that rumor. One of the greats about me. Of course, it's much more interesting for people to think you slept with Picasso than to know you slept with him."

"Indeed. But should a husband know?"

"I should think not," Kitty responded.

"Quite right, dear," George said quietly, while happily turning back to his newspaper.

WIDOW REDUX, AGED 52, 1958

Mrs. George Deen (known as Kitty)

Ex–Collection of Martha and Harrison Whitaker; William
Wallingford III; Luiz Carlos Alfonso Antonio de Braganza;
George Robert Hoppington Deen

In a tragedy of Expressionist intensity, George falls off the
shelf. Careening down the stairs of 990 Fifth Avenue, he
tumbles like a Cy Twombly line and lands as heavy and
unyielding as a Rodin sculpture. Kitty discovers her husband's
tweed-covered mass slumped below its pedestal and knows
that she is alone again. Conservation efforts to restore
George stretch on for a year, but the damage is irreparable,
compromising both structure and function.

STEPMOTHER, AGED 52, 1958

Mrs. George Deen (known as Kitty)
Ex–Collection of Martha and Harrison Whitaker; William
Wallingford III; Luiz Carlos Alfonso Antonio de Braganza;
George Robert Hoppington Deen

Defying funerary traditions, Kitty encounters her stepson
for the first time and seduces him. Sebastian Deen, aged
thirty-nine, had not met Kitty before the memorial service
and relishes this unorthodox carnal tribute to his late father.
After several weeks of Fauve coupling, the pairing is damaged
when Sebastian steals the Braque painting from above Kitty's
fireplace.

"You live here alone, ma'am?"

"Yes, Officer."

"And the person you said stole the painting . . . your stepson . . . this Sebastian Deen fellow . . . he spent the night here?"

"Yes. He's been staying here since his father's memorial service. I barely know the man."

"But he didn't break in? He just left one morning with the painting."

"Exactly."

"You sure you didn't ask him to take the painting somewhere for you?"

"My God, how old do I look?"

"Not a day over twenty-five, ma'am. You say you and Mr. Deen received the painting as a wedding present?"

"No, it was a wedding present from my first marriage. Mr. Deen was my third husband."

"Busy lady."

"Pardon me?"

"It's just . . . well . . . remarkable for a woman as young as you are, ma'am."

"Are you Italian?"

"Yes, ma'am."

"You seem quite charming for an Italian."

"I'm not sure, ma'am."

"I'm quite sure."

SEBASTIAN DEEN
Kitty's Stepson, Aged 39, 1958
Ex–Collection of Fleur and George Hoppington Deen

Swaddled in a bedsheet, the stolen painting sits in Sebastian's suitcase at his hotel. Braque was smug the day he finished the still life, thinking it among his best, and Sebastian echoes that satisfaction. A drink is in order to celebrate the triumph. A looser, freer line delineates Sebastian's steps as he heads east on 56th Street, both distracted and buoyed by his conquest, until a blurred brushstroke washes over his composition. He is run down and killed by the Third Avenue bus.

WINNER, AGED 52, 1958

Mrs. George Deen (known as Kitty)

Ex–Collection of Martha and Harrison Whitaker; William Wallingford III; Luiz Carlos Alfonso Antonio de Braganza; George Robert Hoppington Deen

Long recognized for the sheen of her luster, Kitty beams when the Braque still life returns to her living room. She has grown to love the painting and its stolen words, among them one of her favorites, the French word for "quotidian." It is the ideal categorization for her late stepson: "ordinary, especially when mundane." The abandoned hook above the fireplace receives the painting with the soothing comfort of possession, as the canvas perfectly covers a rectangle of slightly brighter wall paint.

"And so begins another interregnum," Kitty sighed, looking up at her trophy as if talking to Braque himself. It was a singular herald to what she would later refer to as a "duodecennial period" of cold storage.

MELISSA CRANE PORTMAN (KNOWN AS SISSY)
Paragon/Former Bridesmaid, Aged 56, 1962
Collection of James Willoughby Portman (known as Bobo)
Ex–Collection of Clarissa and Buford Crane

A member of Kitty's original garniture, Sissy upholds the
paradigm of WASP manufacturing by producing a balustrade
of two sons and two daughters in precise, evenly spaced,
alternating succession. The Bobo Portmans are now their own
six-piece garniture arranged annually for a portrait that captures
their impeccable composition. As she observes Kitty's sweeping
progression through three husbands, Sissy relishes her superior
status, all while delicately obscuring one minor, asymmetrical
embellishment: Bobo enjoys wearing Sissy's lingerie after the
children go to bed.

WHITNEY STOKES VANDERLOO (KNOWN AS WHIPPY)
Genteel Hoarder/Former Bridesmaid, Aged 57, 1964
Collection of Lincoln Taylor Vanderloo (known as Link)
Ex–Collection of Mary and Bingham Stokes

Whippy sheepishly retreats to a suburban installation that conforms to the Vanderloos' sharply trimmed budget. Much is tarnished in this new linoleum-clad vitrine where Whippy clutches to the surreal decadence of her garniture childhood by saving anything and everything for some indeterminate restoration period. The result is a Pop Art collage of modern consumption, a form of primitive mythmaking in the context of aristocratic exile.

HARRIET PARKER CARTWRIGHT (KNOWN AS CORKIE)
Journalist/Former Bridesmaid, Aged 59, 1966
Ex–Collection of Edith and Winthrop Cartwright III; Thaddeus
Wilson; Walker Grigsby

Maintaining the broad dimensions of her youth, Corkie rejects
her ancestral precedents and Medici wealth to embrace the
radical world of genuine employment. She transforms into
an unflinching journalist and feminist mother with fearlessly
contoured opinions—staunch, muscular, and bold. After two
failed marriages to essentially the same plaster cast man, her
rebellion continues when she begins an affair with her editor.
Their clichéd file-room coupling rubs away any gilding Corkie
may have retained.

CECILIA HUNTINGTON PARRISH (KNOWN AS CECE)
Political Wife/Former Bridesmaid, Aged 61, 1968
Collection of Wheaton Parrish (known as Teddy)
Ex–Collection of Margaret and Russell Huntington

Cece takes on the profile of a monumental footed bowl.
Her thickened silhouette disguises the generation-wide gap
between her and her older husband, who has the tapering
proportions of a slim Georgian candlestick. Though wrought
from solid silver, Teddy cannot ease Cece's strangely lingering
thoughts about Bucky, a long-dead prize she foolishly
relinquished four decades earlier.

PARTY GUEST, AGED 64, 1970
Caroline Margaret Brooks Whitaker Wallingford de Braganza Deen
(known as Kitty)
Ex–Collection of Martha and Harrison Whitaker; William
Wallingford III; Luiz Carlos Alfonso Antonio de Braganza;
George Robert Hoppington Deen

Kitty is on display at the Metropolitan Museum of Art's
Centennial Ball. She revives her jeweled parure, still clogged
in parts with Depression-era frosting. Her conventional profile
stands in contrast to more contemporary forms, ripe and
youthful with their rippling hair and snug gowns. The scent of
late modernist pot in the Great Hall reinforces these stylistic
differences as Kitty clutches her gin and prepares to dodge
Buzzy McClure, a capacious tureen of a man known for his
roving finial.

"Would you care to dance, Mrs. Deen?" the director of the Metropolitan Museum asked.

"Dance? Mr. Hoving, surely there is some young woman with her tits bobbling who you'd prefer to dance with this evening."

"Quite right, Mrs. Deen, but do any of them have an early Braque hanging over their fireplace? I don't think so."

"Oh, how I do appreciate your shamelessness, Tom. I believe this is what Dorothy Parker called being 'trapped like a trap in a trap.'"

(SCHOOL OF) DOCENT, AGED 69, 1976
Caroline Margaret Brooks Whitaker Wallingford de Braganza Deen
(known as Kitty)
Ex–Collection of Martha and Harrison Whitaker; William
Wallingford III; Luiz Carlos Alfonso Antonio de Braganza;
George Robert Hoppington Deen

Facing colossal boredom, Kitty experiments with the construct
of employment. With no apparent skills or financial need, she
secures a position as a docent at the Metropolitan Museum,
without fully considering the public interaction involved.
Kitty's blunt edges do not lend themselves to patient
explanations, causing her hasty reassignment to the European
Paintings Department. After a lengthy lunch with a favorite
curator, Kitty casually wonders if she could tuck a painting
under her coat when she leaves.

FORMER BEAUTY, AGED 70, 1976
Caroline Margaret Brooks Whitaker Wallingford de Braganza Deen
(known as Kitty)
Ex–Collection of Martha and Harrison Whitaker; William
Wallingford III; Luiz Carlos Alfonso Antonio de Braganza;
George Robert Hoppington Deen

In a radical break with tradition, Kitty questions her
masterpiece status. Over lunch, curator Peter Whitney explains
to her the social advantages enjoyed by the truly beautiful—
as if Kitty has never experienced such adoration. The bold
brushwork and scale of his assertion, along with Kitty's marked
absence in his portrait, render her both speechless in her
response and near Cubist in her expression. Kitty tightens her
jaw and leaves with Peter's platinum cigarette case.

ELLEN BARTON

Assistant, Department of European Paintings, The Metropolitan Museum of Art, Aged 23, 1976

Collection of Elizabeth and Joseph Barton (known as Beth and Joe)

Ellen examines the porcelain machinations of Kitty Deen, European Paintings' ostensible volunteer, and catalogues her somewhere between a rigid English tea caddy and a frothy Sèvres vase. A childless woman, Mrs. Deen enjoys the unfettered path of the rich but without any real ambition; she was raised as a prize—a pretty thing entitled to pretty things. While there exists a certain Brutalist daring in knowing there is nothing beyond one's own life, Ellen wonders, does Kitty even dream?

"*What do you mean she steals stuff?*"

"*I don't mean art. I mean just stuff, stuff from around.*"

"*Like what? What would an incredibly wealthy seventy-year-old woman want with any of our stuff?*"

"*Like the other day, I was walking into the outer office, and she was dropping that little origami crane into her purse.*"

"*The thing from the Japanese ambassador? So, a piece of folded paper. Should we call the cops?*"

"*I just think it's weird.*"

"*Rich people are weird. They expect things; they are given things; they possess things. In her case, she possesses a Braque. An early one. And we want it, so let her have the fucking crane if she needs it.*"

DAUGHTER, AGED 70, 1976

*Caroline Margaret Brooks Whitaker Wallingford de Braganza Deen
(known as Kitty)*

Ex–Collection of Martha and Harrison Whitaker; William
Wallingford III; Luiz Carlos Alfonso Antonio de Braganza;
George Robert Hoppington Deen

A deathbed revelation upturns accepted scholarship about
Kitty's provenance. Her mother admits that an alternate
manufacturer collaborated on her production, rendering Kitty
not the daughter of Whit Whitaker, but the output of Digby
Toppinghill. Visual comparison to the concealed progenitor
leaves little room for argument, though a reputation for bland
mediocrity sours this long-dead source. Kitty feels her gilding
dull in the light of her reattribution and indignantly drops her
mother's hand just before her final breath.

DANFORTH GRIGGS TOPPINGHILL (KNOWN AS DIGBY)
(1883–1970)
Progenitor of Caroline Margaret Brooks Whitaker Wallingford de
Braganza Deen (known as Kitty)
Ex–Collection of Pamela and William Griggs Toppinghill
(known as Pip and Coop)

A fine contour ranks Digby as among the most attractive of
his trophy-shaped type. While no qualities of invention or
imagination are brought to bear on his design, his predictably
smooth finish yields a gentle seduction. Barren in her marriage,
a determined Minty Whitaker targeted Digby's curvilinear form
to serve as a studio substitute. Their rhythmic juxtaposition
marked a groundbreaking artistic alliance, though Digby never
knew the generative outcome of their private pairing.

WEDDING GUEST, AGED 71, 1978
Caroline Margaret Brooks Whitaker Wallingford de Braganza Deen
(known as Kitty)
Ex–Collection of Martha and Harrison Whitaker; William
Wallingford III; Luiz Carlos Alfonso Antonio de Braganza;
George Robert Hoppington Deen

With Romanesque restraint, Whippy's granddaughter Penelope
(known as Pip) marries Jeff Moloney in Massapequa, New York.
The bride and groom's sterile demeanor reflects the ceremony
itself: sturdy and plain, to the point of sullen. Kitty notes the
ordinary flowers and discount shoes with a flash of appreciation
for the pristine condition of her own gilding. As she leaves
the church, she pockets a toy car left behind by the growling
ringbearer, a pallid boy with bulging eyes and severed bangs in
the tradition of early Gothic column figures.

TUT VISITOR, AGED 72, 1978
Caroline Margaret Brooks Whitaker Wallingford de Braganza Deen
(known as Kitty)
Ex–Collection of Martha and Harrison Whitaker; William
Wallingford III; Luiz Carlos Alfonso Antonio de Braganza;
George Robert Hoppington Deen

The Metropolitan Museum's King Tut exhibition echoes the
motifs of Kitty's 1925 Egyptian-themed cotillion and recalls the
thrill of her initial pairing with Bucky Wallingford: the harmony
of their robust outlines, the clarity of their imagery, the balance
of their flanking on the eve of his departure to war. The linear
hieroglyphs of that previous era, with its reassuring prosperity
and ornament, are Tut-like in their magnitude. An ancient,
fragmented memory of a boy king and his bride.

NEAR PAIR, AGED 73, 1980

*Caroline Margaret Brooks Whitaker Wallingford de Braganza Deen
(known as Kitty)*

Ex–Collection of Martha and Harrison Whitaker; William
Wallingford III; Luiz Carlos Alfonso Antonio de Braganza;
George Robert Hoppington Deen

While installed in the Metropolitan Museum's porcelain
galleries, Kitty discovers an unlikely companion recently
deaccessioned from the museum's maintenance staff. Of
radically divergent provenance, Larry is all terracotta, notably
unglazed, and without any discernible ornament save a
companionable affection for words. This shared affinity
connects these two empty vessels when they meet daily in
those same galleries to solve the *Times* crossword puzzle. It is
perhaps the first time that Kitty truly feels that her ormolu has
met its match.

LAWRENCE KANDLER
Retired Metropolitan Museum Custodian, Aged 78, 1983
Ex–Collection of Mabel and Irving Kandler (known as Mae
and Irv)

With a disarming frontality and strikingly fluid form, Larry
installs himself daily in the galleries as a ritual comfort.
Juxtaposed with neoclassical Kitty's porcelain craquelure,
he spars quietly with her over nouns and verbs, adjectives
and phrases. After three years, this special exhibition closes
unexpectedly when Larry breaks his hip and cannot reach his
gallery companion. Kitty elegantly waits each day, reminded
of her time in storage during the war, and ultimately resigns
herself to the cyclical calendar of her singular presentation.

"Are you Kitty?"

"Why, yes. Yes, I am," Kitty replied.

"I'm Walter, a friend of Larry's. He asked me to come tell you that he broke his hip, so he can't come to the museum for a while."

"Oh dear. I do hope he's okay."

"Oh, he'll be fine. It's probably his wife who'll suffer the most with Larry home all day." Walter chuckled.

Kitty stiffened. "Well, thank you for the information. It was very kind of you to come."

LEAVER, AGED 82, 1988

Caroline Margaret Brooks Whitaker Wallingford de Braganza Deen (known as Kitty)

Ex–Collection of Martha and Harrison Whitaker; William Wallingford III; Luiz Carlos Alfonso Antonio de Braganza; George Robert Hoppington Deen

With impressionist subtlety, a reversal takes hold. Kitty gathers her collection of purloined objects and distributes them, one by one, to unexpected venues. The owl hatpin is affixed to the back of a collar in the Colony Club cloakroom. The green glass marble casts glowing circles when it is quietly left upon a silver tray in Bootsie Davenport's front hall. Part performance piece, part retrospective, these minimalist installations become Kitty's own tidy addiction.

MOURNER, AGED 85, 1992

Caroline Margaret Brooks Whitaker Wallingford de Braganza Deen (known as Kitty)

Ex–Collection of Martha and Harrison Whitaker; William Wallingford III; Luiz Carlos Alfonso Antonio de Braganza; George Robert Hoppington Deen

With staged solemnity, Kitty reunites with her original garniture when Whippy dies. The exhibition is one of excavated envy, cautiously lacquered with halting sentiment. Edges are now beveled, but still present, and the balance that epitomizes any garniture is definitively undone. Kitty imagines Whippy crated like a fallen caryatid, still proud of her hair, though not quite as thin as Kitty. It does not occur to Kitty that she is measuring herself against an unseen corpse. She leaves a caviar spoon on the casket.

"Remember when Whippy locked Kitty in that commode?" Corkie laughed, reminiscing about that moment so many decades ago. "We must have been what, seven? Kitty used to tell everyone that she trapped Whippy, but I knew better. That Whippy seemed dim, but boy, she could be mean."

"And Kitty wet her pants, tucked up in there," Sissy added through tears of laughter. "I bet if you opened up that cabinet right now, you'd still smell it."

"She had that lisp," Cece said with venom, then mocking, "'Thorry, thorry, thorry . . .' God, I can't believe Bucky Wallingford married her instead of me."

MATRON, AGED 91, 1998

Caroline Margaret Brooks Whitaker Wallingford de Braganza Deen (known as Kitty)

Ex–Collection of Martha and Harrison Whitaker; William Wallingford III; Luiz Carlos Alfonso Antonio de Braganza; George Robert Hoppington Deen

Kitty's glaze has yellowed, hardened after too many years on display. Beneath a perfectly stiffened crown, every joint and tendon flexes. Bones are stacked like wooden blocks, not a single swag interrupting their rigid architecture, anchored by the parallel position of her sensibly, expensively clad feet. Fastened with buttoned-wool precision, pressed into austere luxury, Kitty clutches her purse preventatively, as if a mugging is already in progress. So much has been stolen from her.

A DOG NAMED BABY
Pug, Aged 16, 1999
Ex–Collection of Mrs. Prudence Palmer Farnsworth
(known as Bim)
On loan

A startling addition softens Kitty's hard-paste porcelain when
she informally adopts a dead neighbor's dog, oddly named Baby.
The overweight pug ignores Kitty's flaws with affecting head
tilts and gentle nudges. Kitty denies this kindness and assumes
the dog has simply mistaken one old vessel for another. It is
only when Kitty collapses and Baby frantically licks her that she
registers the dog's loyalty. Baby still winces remembering the
acrid taste of Kitty's bisque surface.

"Good morning. We're here from the Metropolitan Museum to pick up a painting from Mrs. Deen's apartment."

"Jeez. We just lost her yesterday," Kitty's doorman replied.

"Her will instructed that the painting be collected within twenty-four hours. I believe Mrs. Deen's lawyer is already upstairs. I suspect she was concerned about theft."

"C'mon in," the doorman instructed. "Funny lady, that Mrs. Deen. She once called me pulchritudinous. I had to look it up. Last year, she put a little silver fork in the envelope with my Christmas tip . . . not sure why. Nice lady, though . . ."

ROSARIO CANDELA (1890–1953)
Kitty's Vitrine, 1927–1999, 990 Fifth Avenue, Floors 10 and 11
Limestone, steel, wood, marble, 1927
Collection of Mrs. George Deen

A Candela masterpiece of classical proportions, the duplex
feels like a museum period room devoted to twentieth-century
patrician wealth. A fragile atmosphere crackles within the
apartment, a sense of some long-ago happiness purposely
trapped in its walls for safekeeping. That joy, so carefully
collected and tenderly curated, now seeps from the gaps around
the old windows. The Braque still life hangs in a dusty cone of
light, both treasure and trophy.

"Did we know she had a Picasso here too?"

"No, we definitely did not know she had a Picasso here too."

"Why would she tape it to the back of the Braque? You think she stole it? She was notorious for pinching things."

"Did Kitty Deen steal a Picasso? Please. But there've always been rumors that she had some kind of affair with him. I never believed them. . . . It's much later than the Braque, midcentury, maybe late 1940s with that brushwork."

"So, who gets it? Can we take it back to the museum?"

"Sotheby's and Christie's have probably known about it for years. Go find that lawyer."

PABLO PICASSO (1881–1973)
Still Life with Vase
Oil on canvas, 1950
Gift of Mrs. George Deen
1999.23.2

A strange fragility marks this striking canvas. Painted during a brief trip to England in 1950, the still life retains Picasso's Cubist compositional methods while employing the bold line that is typical of the period. The deliberate isolation of the subject and aggressively foreshortened space encourage a sense of tenuous stability, a solidity that may soon be upended, causing the vase to crash to the floor.

"... *This recently acquired 1950 Picasso still life maintains the seminal impetus of the movement. Cubism introduced the very idea of the simultaneity of time, and the concept of the fragmentary standing for the whole. For Picasso and Braque, it was a game, a sleight of hand. The painting is both an insufficient glimpse of its subject and everything you need to know about it. In a late poem, artist Meret Oppenheim speaks of 'an enormously tiny bit of a lot.' Likewise, in the Cubist world, a sliver can conjure an entire form, complete and unbroken. Our eye, our mind, our imagination, are left to fill in what is missing. And what a pleasure it is to do so.*"

Professor Bertram McWhittle concluding his lecture "Cubism and the Imagination" at The Metropolitan Museum of Art, 1999

GHOST, AGED 117, 2023

Caroline Margaret Brooks Whitaker Wallingford de Braganza Deen (known as Kitty)

Ex–Collection of Martha and Harrison Whitaker; William Wallingford III; Luiz Carlos Alfonso Antonio de Braganza; George Robert Hoppington Deen

I am wrapped, crated, and covered, kept in the depths of an eternal warehouse. The ancient legacy of a type and a time, pulled from display because of lack of relevance, lack of interest, lack of edge, lack of struggle, lack of story. I will float through the world for a thousand years until they wonder about my type again. A classical form. A marrying kind. A childless woman. Once flawless, inevitable. Now broken, irrelevant. Chipped, cracked, and packed away.

ACKNOWLEDGMENTS

I am the furthest thing from a one woman show.

I remain grateful to everyone at the Metropolitan Museum of Art who let me write quietly for twenty-five years so that I could write loudly now. I am particularly indebted to curators Luke Syson and Ellenor Alcorn, who commissioned me to write labels for The Met's British Galleries, where the idea for this novel was born.

Three extraordinary women supported me in the book's earliest days: my magnificent agent Elisabeth Weed and firecracker editors Hilary Leichter and Catherine Nichols. Super reader Steven Estok joined their ranks later and only ever saw possibilities.

Encouragement takes many forms—conversations, questions, doubt, delight—and I thank the following people for joining this somewhat questionable endeavor during its many different stages: Doon Arbus, Julie Barer, Deeda Blair, Barbara Boehm, Liz Bowyer, Julie Burstein, Anne Dickerson, John Dickerson, Maira Kalman, Peter Mendelsund, Lisa Naftolin, Christopher Noey, Russell Piccione, Dolores Rice, Rosemarie Ryan, Neil Selkirk, Leanne Shapton, Andrew Solomon, and Stephen Yorke.

I am also grateful for my time at the American Academy in Rome where I was able to finish Kitty's story.

The remarkable Ben Loehnen, vice president and editor in chief at Avid Reader Press, will forever be known to me as "bananas brilliant" for his initial response to the manuscript. I could not have asked for a better or more delightful champion for this book. Alison Forner, Yvette Grant, Allison Green, Katherine Hernández, Carolyn Kelly, Carly Loman, Caroline McGregor, Alex Primiani, Meredith Vilarello, Lauren Wein, Barbara Wild, and the entire team at Simon & Schuster were wonderful and clever and endlessly patient with an author who cares about *everything*. Publicist Kate Lloyd and foreign rights agent Jenny Meyer are simply marvels. In London, the great Josephine Greywoode, publishing director at Penguin Random House UK, brought nothing but unbridled enthusiasm to her release of *One Woman Show*.

The genius of Dorothy Parker deserves a nod for obvious influence in Kitty's early chatter, and the real dog named Baby belongs to the splendid Kate Chartener. And finally, to my three Cs, who let me correct their grammar and talk about verbs at dinner: Every word is always for you.

ABOUT THE AUTHOR

Christine Coulson spent twenty-five years writing for the Metropolitan Museum of Art and left as Senior Writer in 2019. Her debut novel about the museum, *Metropolitan Stories*, was a national bestseller.